Is That You, Winter?

A STORY BY STEPHEN GAMMELL

SCHOLASTIC INC.   New York   Toronto   London   Auckland   Sydney   Mexico City   New Delhi   Hong Kong

As usual, Old Man Winter
wakes up in a bad mood.

With no time for breakfast,
he hurries outside.

And, once again, he's off!

High above,
Winter lets loose
his icy blast.

Cold wind
whips the snow
through the freezing air.

Wintertime is here.

But sometimes
Old Man Winter is puzzled.

Cold and tired
from the morning's work,
he's ready for lunch.

But the snow is too deep
for Old Man Winter,
and he tumbles to the ground.

Some children are playing in the backyard.
One little girl hears him land.

"Hey, Winter!"

She picks him up and makes sure that he's all right.

"HE'S OLD MAN WINTER, MY FRIEND... AND HE'S NOT RATTY!"

Seeing that he's safe on the steps,
she runs back to play with her friends
in the snow that fell this morning.

And, once more,

Old Man Winter is in a good mood.

A BOOK FOR LINDA

ISBN 0-590-20028-3

The illustrations in this book were done in pastels, pencils, and watercolor on Lana Pur Fil printmaking paper.
The display type was hand-lettered by the illustrator. The text type was set in Galliard.

12 11 10 9 8 7 6 5 4 3 2 1   8 9/9 0 1 2 3/0

Printed in the U.S.A.   14

First Scholastic printing, November 1998